MUSINGS OF AN IDLE MIND

ISLET FROM THE OCEAN OF THOUGHTS

ANANYA SAXENA

Contents

CHAPTER ONE

THE MOON TOLD ME SO

Lying down on soft grass, under the tree,

on knolls dissolving into the meadow,

I look at the starlit night,When the sky's smile catches my eye,

The moon stood out, huge and painfully bright,

it wore an amused and mocking smile.

I turned my eyes and mind to the tree under which I rested

"Your leaves dance in the wind, they help you live and then they leave you," I said.

"They leave me because they know that a new generation is to rise and to replace their purpose, the past must give way for new, but I can never forget any of them just because they are gone," the Tree replied.

After long hours of dreary silence, I was delighted to talk to someone, so I asked the Tree in curiosity, "Your roots hold you firm to the ground, prohibiting you to move and explore the world, do you ever get mad?"

"Never! My roots give me life, and I in turn give life to others, what is it to me to mourn over something I cannot do? No amount of traveling can replace the feeling I have when birds perch on my branches at dawn and sing their songs or when a busy squirrel makes its winter home in my trunk," the Tree answered.

I turned to the ground on which I lay and asked, "So many feet trod over you, yet you remain calm, how?"

"I am the witness of the first life's creation and its destruction, I have seen creatures evolve. I have a long way to go as I am the Ground on which the Past, Present and Future walk. I do not mind being walked on by my children as my duty is to protect them from Earth's fiery interior," the Ground replied tenderly.

A gust of wind shook the leaves of the Tree, so I asked it, " You have witnessed the past and carry life within you like the Tree and the Ground. You are like invisible water in which we are floating. Have you ever questioned your purpose?"

"I have, but then I look at the creatures into which I breathe life, to see their faces looking at their surroundings with such innocent curiosity. We who sustain life on Earth work as a team," the Wind majestically replied.

My throat felt parched, so I walked to nearest well, thinking over the answers given to me that had changed my perspective. I reached my destination and drew up a bucket of water. After quenching my thirst, I peered into the well and asked the water, "Have you ever wished to disappear or forget the past?"

"If I disappear, it will not be possible for life to exist. I have been discouraged but on seeing the life I behold and the life whom I give relief to, I find myself smiling at the thought of seeing them smile. As for the past, forgetting it wouldn't be possible, it teaches us important lessons and reminds us of people that never leave us," replied the Water with a cool composure.

I strolled back to my shelter under the Tree, and after regaining my seat, I leaned against its trunk. I looked back at the Moon. Its smile had grown brighter and looked at me even more mockingly than before. So, I finally asked it with some asperity, "What pleasure do you get laughing at me?"

"I do not laugh at you but at all of humankind. You claim to be getting smarter and I ask if that is the case then why are you indirectly repeating history?" replied the Moon in its clear deep voice.

A few moments lapsed in silence till I asked the moon, "Can anyone change the lasting effects and consequences of the past?"

"No, but the future can be changed, if decisions of the present are taken wisely," replied the Moon.

Now I looked at the Moon, it no longer looked harsh but kind and benevolent. As I sat looking at the twinkling stars,

I heard the Water in distant well splashing with rage, the Ground quivered, the Tree under which I had taken shelter, shook violently, the Wind roared, I saw the sky shrinking, the Moon waving 'goodbye', and felt the cold fresh air turn warmer and warmer.

I jumped awake on my bed, looked around my room, dazed, then stared outside the window through which the golden rays of sunlight had slipped into the room and saw the Tree swaying in breeze, seeming to say "goodbye my dear friend!"

CHAPTER TWO

THE PITTER-PATTER OF RAIN

Now she sits on a rocking chair by the window, looking out through it. She still sees a busy street on a rainy- groggy day. The pitter-patter of the raindrops on the window glass takes her back to her childhood. It was somewhat a similar day- a dull and busy day at the house near the woods where they lived. It was heavy rain that verged on a rainstorm. Two children played with paper boats in a puddle of water outside the backdoor. As she takes this calm and steady stroll down the memory lane, she looks at the tapestry hanging on one of the walls. She notices the beautiful moose she had seen years ago, in the woods, not far from her home.

It was yet another rainy day…also a day of mourning. She had wandered into the woods, at break of the dawn, crying hopelessly, when her eyes caught a movement in the bushes. She saw a magical magnificent creature stumble out of it. It was a white moose with golden antlers. They developed a remarkable bond. They protected and took care of each other. They became an irreplaceable part of each other's life. She would walk into the woods filled with life and spend hours there. She felt safe, free and happy there. From the day she left those woods, she felt empty. At times, the moose began to appear randomly! It didn't make sense, not that she cared! She was with a friend who cared and reciprocated her affection. Whether she was in a busy city or the calm countryside, the moose was always close by, sometimes afraid of the crowd. It was only in those deep woods that both of them felt free. Free to dream, feel and to be themselves. She sat meditating in this pool of thoughts, when she realized that the rain had stopped. She opened the window and a gust of cool air entered the room. The room filled up with purple and blue swirls of mist and the moose emerged from the cloud of glitter.

She stood up and reached the moose and stroked it gently. At that time, they both felt as free as they had felt in the woods. I haven't seen her since. This story is as true and real as you and I. Now you must be wondering, "who am I and how do I know this?" Well my dear! I am the wind, a witness to everything and I have not seen such a beautiful and unique friendship ever since.

CHAPTER THREE

MUSINGS OF AN IDLE MIND

What is an emotion?
An embellishment of civilized life,
A boon and curse of existence.
What is love?
A guiding star of life.
What is a heart-break?
A consequence of the power of attachment
Within the sweet nectar of life
Lies also the bitter fragments of being.
To sink slowly into a sea of bliss and
be nibbled at by the devil of resentment.
What is life?
To live in a house with frail walls
That collapse during the approach
Of a terrifying storm.
To find courage
To smile at the face of terror
And embrace the pieces
While making a better, stronger home.
That is life.

DIAMONDS OF PRESENCE

I sat there with them
Then in the blink of an eye
That present turned into the past
The diamonds left by their presence
Embedded in someone's heart.
The diamonds made of those people's memories and presence
Lies scattered in different corners of the world.
It grows and divides
As rhythmic and systematic as a heartbeat.
The people whose faces never fade from memory
their effect and influence on a fond heart never withers.
The memory of those loved souls no longer with us
acts as a steady flickering flame in a river of sadness.
Now those present will rise in the morning to become the past
All in a part of the method of life.
To go forward, leave someone unwillingly
To leave someone is to wait to be left by them.
The silent words of hope that we meet again
Get drowned again and again into the river of doubt or are
Blown away by winds of resentment endlessly.
Nevertheless, we pray, that
if effortlessly we can turn people into memories and
even more turn into memories,
Then maybe life could be less heavy.

CHAPTER FIVE

DEARLY BELOVED

For every time you cried,
every time you felt vulnerable to pain.
Whenever you rest your sword for an instance
in the battle to relieve your burden.
I wish I am by your side.
In spirit, mind and heart
I wish you to taste the golden fruit
While I stand between you and the bed of nails.
If I can I would absorb your pain and hurt
To give what you deserve-absolute heaven.
I fear my love for you, you shall not see
Its depths deeper than the deepest well
And its strength, stronger than the strongest rope.
I fear you should not see your value
For your presence to me is more than all the
Riches and luxuries the world has to offer.
I wish to absorb all your pain, your hurt
And when you rest to catch your breath, to regain your strength.
I'll be by your side, your pillar of support
And strain you to my heart and set you forward
Filled with love and hope onwards towards your battle.
And when you or I finish our fights,
I'll remember forever the mark you left in my heart.

CHAPTER SIX

AN ISLET FROM THE OCEAN OF THOUGHT

The power of words,
just like tides,
to move or to destroy.
Spoken, unspoken,
written, unwritten,
may become a sweet nectarous anecdote,
or a lethal unsavory poison.
Thus let your library of diction,
be marked with caution,
every word of every thought,
when blossoms cannot be undone.
So hence give yourself,
some respect and importance,
hear not and speak not,
all that deserves no thought,
no space in your mind
In the sea of arising confusion,
at least let words be true,
like beacons of light, pious and pure.

CHAPTER SEVEN

RUTH'S RUE

The busy bee has no time for sorrow! There are countless such people but one has the most right to this statement. How many years have passed...decades, centuries? All have gone and piled themselves in rubble. Many people have seen the changes occur and conveniently placed them on the farthest shelf of their memory.

Alas, not all have the pleasure of putting behind their past and living a future as joyous as a blooming rose. Ruth is this person's everlasting name. A name that changes faces but never its memories. She has lived exactly as many years as you and me but still is the oldest soul to have ever ventured.

Year after year, she is born sometimes as a beggar woman, other times as a business tycoon. All this time carrying the burden of memories of people, she can no longer talk to or see. Year after year, this list grows. She sees those she loves but they see her as a mere stranger.

Maybe, she thinks of it as a curse for her but God himself carefully crafted her existence so as to make her the most noble creature to have graced the earth. She was the epitome of change, a symbol for progress to an exulting and exuberant future far from the fairytales and closer to a child's dream.

Now, if she knew this or not, she carried out every action with as much precision as God had imagined. In cities of gold cooled by winds of serenity, where everything is just and everyone is loved; where the modern mixes with primitive, that is where her soul rests. Aching with the pain of the physical world held together by the universe. Her heart is filled with sorrow... with memories of her mothers, fathers, siblings, friends and other kin. But she can never stop to express her pain, for her duty is such that the busy bee has no time for sorrow and Progress can never stop for good and evil.

CHAPTER EIGHT

CAMELLIA BLOOMS

With the days gone by,
with years fading into each other,
how beautifully the Flower blooms.
How beautiful does it look!
among the brambles and the undergrowth,
thriving in the Garden of Life,
surrounded by the sweet chirpings of all things bright and right,
all tangled up with the hisses of idiocracy and vulgarity.
It glows brighter yet,
if you have the courage to change and harvest your energy,
to invest in the fairer prospects.
If you muster up the strength,
to pull yourself out of the mud,
and pay no heed to the thorny bushes,
the Flower's glow will lead you through the way.
And maybe, just maybe,
you will find the balance,
and enjoy your stay,
and stay long enough to see,
that the flower is a reflection of yourself in its glass petals.